W9-BOP-409

Let's Play Tag!

Read the Page

Read the Story

Repeat

Stop

Game

| Level 1 | Level 2 | Level 3 |

Yes

No

INTERNET CONNECTION REQUIRED FOR AUDIO DOWNLOAD.

To use this book with the Tag™ Reader you must download audio from the LeapFrog® Connect Application.
The LeapFrog Connect Application can be installed from the CD provided with your Tag Reader or at leapfrog.com/tag.

To my cousins at Sandbanks - Giles
For Fi, John, Rod, and Andy - Guy

GIRAFFES CAN'T DANCE

by Giles Andreae
illustrated by Guy Parker-Rees

Scholastic Inc.   Orchard Books

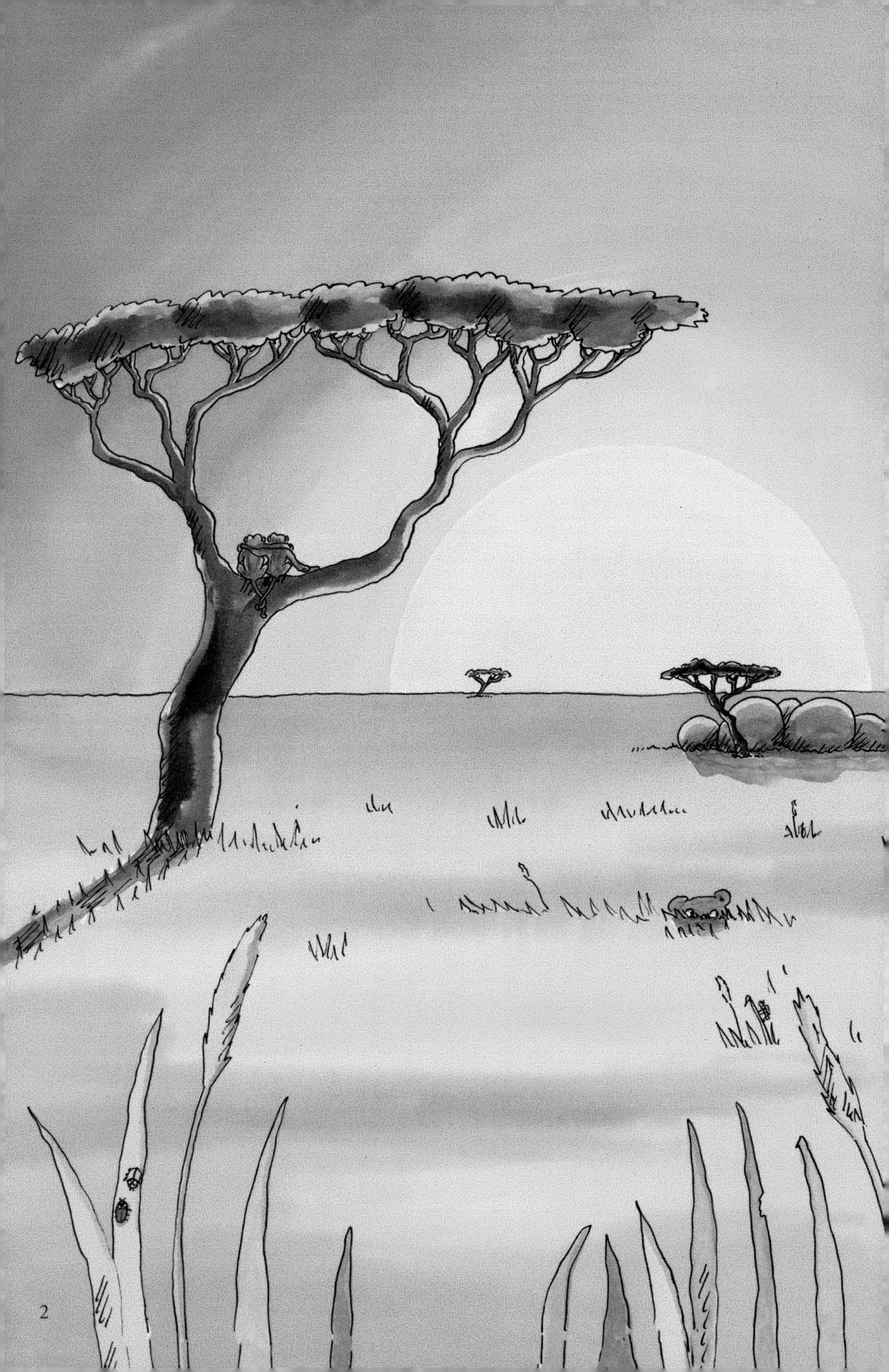

Gerald was a tall giraffe
whose neck was long and slim.
But his knees were awfully crooked
and his legs were rather thin.

3

He was very good at standing still
and munching shoots off trees.

But when he tried to run around,

he buckled at the knees.

Now every year in Africa
they hold the Jungle Dance,
where every single animal
turns up to skip and prance.

JUNGLE DANCE

And this year when the day arrived
poor Gerald felt so sad,
because when it came to dancing
he was really very bad.

The warthogs started waltzing

and the rhinos rock 'n' rolled.

8

The lions danced a tango
that was elegant and bold.

The chimps all did a cha-cha
with a very Latin feel,

and eight baboons then teamed up

for a splendid Scottish reel.

11

Gerald swallowed bravely
as he walked toward the floor.
But the lions saw him coming,
and they soon began to roar.

"Hey, look at clumsy Gerald,"
the animals all sneered.
"Giraffes can't dance, you silly fool!
Oh, Gerald, you're so weird."

Gerald simply froze up.
He was rooted to the spot.
They're right, he thought. *I'm useless.*
Oh, I feel like such a clot.

So he crept off from the dance floor,
and he started walking home.
He'd never felt so sad before –
so sad and so alone.

Then he found a little clearing,
and he looked up at the sky.
"The moon can be so beautiful,"
he whispered with a sigh.

"Excuse me!" coughed a cricket
who'd seen Gerald earlier on.
"But sometimes when you're different
you just need a different song."

"Listen to the swaying grass
and listen to the trees.
To me the sweetest music
is those branches in the breeze.

So imagine that the lovely moon
is playing just for you—
everything makes music
if you really want it to."

19

With that, the cricket smiled
and picked up his violin.
Then Gerald felt his body
do the most amazing thing.

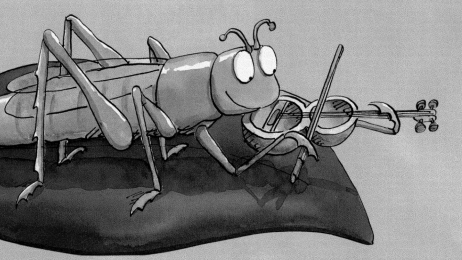

His hooves had started shuffling,
making circles on the ground.
His neck was gently swaying,
and his tail was swishing round.

He threw his legs out sideways,
and he swung them everywhere.
Then he did a backward somersault
and leapt up in the air.

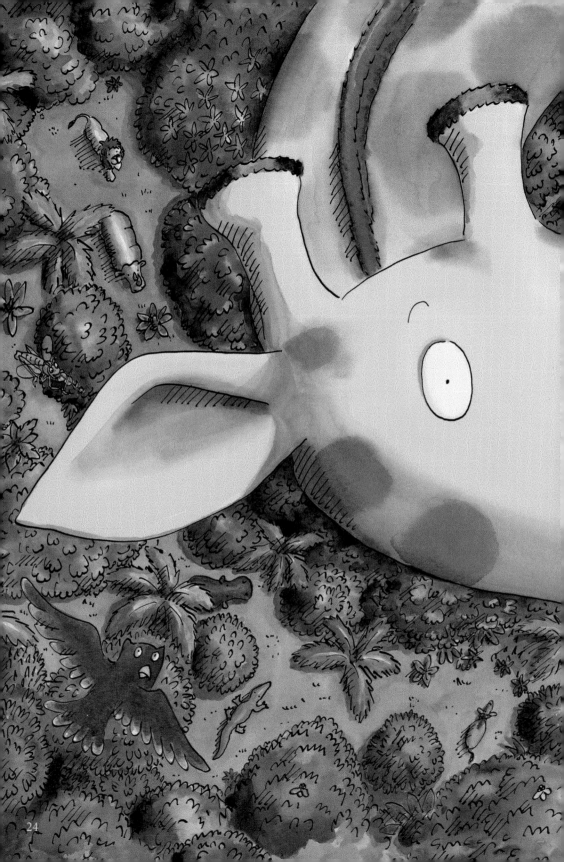

Gerald felt so wonderful
his mouth was open wide.
"I am dancing! Yes, I'm dancing!
I AM *DANCING*!" Gerald cried.

Then, one by one, each animal
who'd been there at the dance
arrived while Gerald boogied on
and watched him, quite entranced.

They shouted, "It's a miracle!
We must be in a dream.
Gerald's the best dancer
that we've ever, ever seen!"

"How did you learn to dance like that?
Please, Gerald, tell us how."
But Gerald simply twirled around
and finished with a bow.

Then he raised his head and looked
up at the moon and stars above.
"We all can dance," he said,
"when we find music that we love."

Jungle Jam

violin   trumpet   maracas
bass   saxophone   bongos
guitar   flute   xylophone

balloon

star

guitar

tree

drum

grapes

mango

cake

plum

Move and Groove

moon

tango

bee

snake

apes